IT'S NOT ABOUT THE
BEANSTALK!

Veronika Martenova Charles

Illustrated by David Parkins

TUNDRA BOOKS

Published in Canada by Tundra Books, a division of Random House of Canada Limited,
One Toronto Street, Suite 300, Toronto, Ontario M5C 2V6

Published in the United States by Tundra Books of Northern New York,
P.O. Box 1030, Plattsburgh, New York 12901

Library of Congress Control Number: 2012945436

Library and Archives Canada Cataloguing in Publication

Charles, Veronika Martenova
    It's not about the beanstalk! / Veronika Martenova Charles ; illustrated
by David Parkins.

(Easy-to-read wonder tales)
Short stories based on Jack and the beanstalk tales from around the world.
ISBN 978-1-77049-327-8. – ISBN 9781770493322 (EPUB)

    1. Fairy tales. I. Parkins, David II. Title. III. Series: Charles, Veronika
Martenova. Easy-to-read wonder tales.

PS8555.H42242I83326 2013   jC813'.54   C2012-905312-0

We acknowledge the financial support of the Government of Canada through the
Canada Book Fund and that of the Government of Ontario through the Ontario Media
Development Corporation's Ontario Book Initiative. We further acknowledge the support of
the Canada Council for the Arts and the Ontario Arts Council for our publishing program.

 ONTARIO ARTS COUNCIL
CONSEIL DES ARTS DE L'ONTARIO

Edited by Stacey Roderick

www.tundrabooks.com

Printed and bound in China

1 2 3 4 5 6   18 17 16 15 14 13

CONTENTS

IN THE YARD
PART 1

"Can Jake come out to play?"

Lily and Ben asked Jake's mother.

"Sure," she replied.

"He's in the backyard."

Jake was throwing a rope

over a tree branch.

"What are you doing?" asked Lily.

"I want to climb up," said Jake.

"Maybe there's a giant's house

where I'll find a treasure."

"Oh," said Ben.

"Like in *Jack and the Beanstalk*."

"It wasn't a beanstalk," said Jake.

"It was a bean tree!"

"There's no such thing," said Lily.

"Sure there is. Listen," said Jake.

THE BEAN TREE

(*Jack and the Beanstalk* from

Appalachia)

One day, while Jack's mother

was sweeping up their cottage,

Jack kept getting in her way.

She picked up a bean from the floor

and said, "Jack, go and plant this."

So Jack ran outside

and planted it under his window.

The next morning, he looked out.

He couldn't believe his eyes!

The bean had grown into a tree

so tall, Jack couldn't see its top!

I'll climb that tree

to see where it goes, he thought.

He climbed up, up, and up

until he reached the top.

There he found a strange,

desert-like land with sand dunes

and cactus plants.

He saw an old woman

walking toward him.

"Hello, Jack," the woman said.

"I'm your godmother," she said.

"It was me who made the bean grow.

Did your mother ever tell you

about your father?"

"No," replied Jack.

"But she always gets sad

when I ask about him."

"Your father was a good man,"

the woman said.

"He was killed by a giant

who had stolen his treasure.

Only you can get it back."

"What do I do?" asked Jack.

"Keep on walking," she replied,

"and you'll see the giant's house.

Just remember the word 'water'!"

So Jack walked until

he came to a big mansion.

It was surrounded

by a wall of cactus plants.

"Stop! What is the password?"

asked the biggest cactus,

as it raised its spiky arms.

Suddenly, Jack remembered.

"Water!" he called out.

"You can pass," the cactus said

and let him through.

A woman stood by the door.

"May I stay the night?" asked Jack.

"You better go back to where

you came from," the woman said.

"My husband is a giant,

and he eats humans.

But I'll hide you just for tonight."

And she hid Jack in the oven.

That night, the giant came home.

"FEE, FI, FO, FUM," he roared.

"I smell the blood of a human."

"Oh, dear," said his wife,

"you're mistaken. It's the lamb

I cooked for your dinner."

After the giant had eaten,

he called, "Bring me my hen!"

His wife placed it on the table.

"Lay!" ordered the giant, and

the hen laid an egg of pure gold.

That must be my father's treasure!

thought Jack.

After the giant had amused himself,

he fell asleep by the fireside.

Jack crept out of the oven

and picked up the hen.

But just as he did, a little dog

that Jack hadn't seen before

started to bark.

The giant stirred.

Jack saw a bone on the table

and threw it to the dog.

Then he grabbed the hen and ran.

Soon he felt the ground shaking.

The giant was chasing him!

Jack reached the bean tree.

He jumped on the trunk

and slid down, down, down.

Above him, the giant hollered.

As Jack touched the ground,

he yelled, "Mom! Bring the ax!"

His mother came running

and handed him the ax.

Chop! Chop! Chop!

Jack hit the tree hard.

The tree started to lean.

Then it crashed across the fields.

BOOM!

The giant fell to the ground

and died.

After it was all quiet,

Jack told his mom what happened

and gave her the magic hen.

From then on, Jack and his mother

never had to worry about a thing,

and they lived happily.

"I wonder what happened to

the giant's wife," said Lily.

"She was nice to Jack."

"She must have felt lonely

when the giant didn't come back,"

said Jake. "But she didn't like

that he ate people."

"I know a story about a boy

who took a treasure from a troll,"

said Ben.

"What's a troll?" asked Jake.

"It's a kind of giant," Ben replied.

"I'll tell you the story."

OLAF AND THE TROLL

(*Jack and the Beanstalk* from

Norway)

Once there was a poor man

who had three sons.

When he died,

the two older brothers

decided to leave their home

and look for work.

"Can I come with you?"

asked Olaf, the youngest one.

"No!" his brothers told him.

"You're fit for nothing.

You could never get a job."

Then the two set off

and found work

in the palace kitchen.

After a while, Olaf set off, too,

taking his father's boat,

which his brothers had left behind.

Olaf also arrived at the palace

and asked if they would hire him.

At first, they didn't want Olaf,

but when he pleaded, they let him

carry the water for the maid.

Olaf was quick and friendly,

and everybody liked him.

His brothers noticed

and grew very jealous of him.

Just opposite the palace,

across another lake,

lived a troll

who had seven silver ducks.

Everybody knew

that the king wanted them.

The brothers told the cook,

"Our brother, Olaf,

said he could catch those ducks."

It wasn't long before

the king found out.

The king sent for Olaf.

"I've heard that you can get

the silver ducks," he told him.

"Go now and fetch them!"

Olaf couldn't argue with the king.

He asked for a bag of seeds

and said he'd try his best.

Olaf loaded the bag into his boat,

and rowed across the lake.

When he reached the other side,

he sprinkled the seeds on the shore.

As the ducks came near,

Olaf caught them

and put them in his boat.

Quickly, he began to row back.

When he was halfway there,

the troll came out and roared,

"Is that *you* who took my ducks?"

"Yes!" Olaf called back.

"Will you be back?"

"Very likely!" answered Olaf.

Olaf brought the ducks to the king,

and the king was very pleased.

"Well done!" he said.

After that, Olaf was liked

even more than before.

His brothers grew more envious.

Once again, they went to the cook

and said, "Our brother told us

he could get the golden harp

that is heard when the wind blows

across the lake."

The cook told others,

and soon the king found out.

The king called Olaf and said,

"I hear that you can get

that golden harp. Bring it to me!"

Again Olaf rowed across the lake.

But *this* time the troll caught him

and took him to his cave.

Olaf saw the golden harp

leaning by the door.

The troll called to his daughter,

"Put this boy in a cage.

Tomorrow you will roast him,

while I invite some friends

to the feast."

The next day, after the troll left,

the daughter lit the fire

and took out a knife.

"Is that what you're going to

cut me with?" asked Olaf.

"Yes, it is," said the daughter.

"But it isn't sharp," said Olaf.

"Let me sharpen it for you.

You'll find it easier to work with."

The daughter opened the cage.

Olaf came out, pushed *her* inside,

and locked it.

Then he grabbed the golden harp

and ran to the shore with it.

He jumped into his boat.

Quickly, he rowed across the lake.

Just then, the troll came back

and saw Olaf on the water.

"Hey!" he roared. "Is that *you*

who took my silver ducks?"

"Yes!" called Olaf.

"And now you have taken my harp?"

"Yes!" replied Olaf.

"Didn't my daughter roast you?"

the troll screeched.

"I guess not!" called Olaf.

When the troll heard that,

he was so angry, he burst!

Olaf returned to the palace

and gave the king the harp.

The king made him his adviser.

Olaf forgave his two brothers,

and, grateful, their jealousy

changed to admiration.

★ ★ ★

"That reminds me of a story

about a girl and her sisters,"

said Lily. "She also had to get

something from a giant

and bring it to a king."

"What was it? Silver ducks?"

asked Ben.

"No," replied Lily.

"I'll tell you the story."

MOLLY AND THE GIANT

(*Jack and the Beanstalk* from
  Scotland)

There was once a man

who had many children

but couldn't feed them all.

One day, he took the three youngest

and left them in the woods.

The children walked and walked

until they came to a house.

The youngest one, named Molly,

knocked on the door.

A woman answered and asked,

"What do you want?"

"Something to eat, please!"

answered Molly.

"Go away," said the woman.

"My husband is a giant.

If he sees you, he'll *eat* you!"

"But we're so tired,"

said the other two girls.

So the woman let them in and

gave them each a piece of bread.

They had just taken a bite

when the giant came home.

"Oh! What have we here?"

the giant asked.

"Three lost and tired girls,"

said his wife.

"I made you a big supper,

so leave the girls to me.

They will sleep here tonight."

Now, the giant had three daughters

of his own, and his wife put

all six girls into the same bed.

The giant went to say good night.

Pretending to play,

he hung gold necklaces

around his daughters' necks.

Then he put straw ropes

around the necks

of Molly and her sisters.

How strange, thought Molly.

When everyone was asleep,

Molly crept across the bed

and switched the necklaces.

Now she and her sisters wore

the gold ones, and the giant's

daughters wore the straw ropes.

In the middle of the night,

the giant came into the room

and felt the girls' necks.

He plucked out the girls with

the straw ropes and

carried them down to the cellar.

"I'll have them for breakfast,"

he said to himself.

As soon as it was quiet again,

Molly woke up her sisters.

"We must get out of here,"

she whispered. "Right now!"

The girls slipped out of the house

and stumbled through the darkness.

At sunrise, they came to a canyon.

Far below, a river ran wildly.

There was a long strand of hair

spanning it like a bridge.

"We have to cross,"

said Molly to her sisters.

"But how can we?" they asked.

"Let me try first," said Molly.

She climbed up,

balanced herself, and walked.

"We can do it! The hair is magic!"

Molly shouted to her sisters.

She helped each of them across.

On the other side of the canyon

stood a big castle

that belonged to a king.

Molly went in

and told the king her story.

"You're very brave," the king said.

"That giant stole my father's sword.

If you bring it back to me,

I'll reward you with a house

and all the food you want."

"I'll try," said Molly.

She returned to the giant's house,

and at night she sneaked inside.

The sword hung by the giant's bed.

Slowly, Molly took it off.

CLANG! The sword fell down.

"Now I've got you!" the giant roared.

"Tell me, girl, if I were you,

how would you punish me?"

"I would put you in a sack and

hang you on the wall," said Molly.

"Then I'd cut a stick in the woods,

come back, and beat you to a jelly."

"Well," laughed the giant,

"that's exactly what I'll do to you."

He put Molly into a sack

and went out to find a stick.

Molly started singing,

If you could see what I see!

"What is it?" asked the giant's wife.

"I can't describe it," Molly said.

"It's *sooo* beautiful!"

"Please let me look,"

the wife begged.

She let Molly out of the bag

and climbed inside herself.

At once, Molly grabbed the sword

and ran back to the palace.

When the giant returned,

his wife told him Molly escaped.

He flew into a rage.

"I'll catch that girl!" he screamed.

The giant ran after Molly

through the woods.

He was catching up

when they reached the canyon

with the magic strand of hair.

Molly skipped along over it,

but the giant would not dare.

Molly arrived at the castle

and gave the sword to the king.

The king kept his promise.

He had a big house built for Molly

and her sisters and made sure

they never went hungry again.

IN THE YARD
PART 2

"I'm going to climb the tree now,"

Jake told Lily and Ben.

He jumped up, grabbing the rope.

THUMP!

Jake fell as the rope slipped off.

Jake's mom came outside.

"What happened?" she asked.

"I'm okay," said Jake and got up.

"I just forgot to tie the rope!"

"Mom," Jake asked,

"are there bean *trees*?"

"Yes, there are," she replied.

"I know there are

chocolate bean trees."

"Wow! Can we plant one

in our yard?" asked Jake.

"We could grow chocolate bars."

"Those trees need a different

climate," said Jake's mom.

"And you don't *eat* those beans.

Chocolate is made from their seeds."

"Mom," said Jake,

"do *you* have any chocolate?"

"I'll take a look," she laughed.

In a minute, she came back.

"All I could find are

these jelly beans," she said.

"Thanks, Mom!" Jake said,

holding them in his hand.

"Aren't you sharing?" asked Ben.

"Sure," said Jake.

"But what if we plant these beans

and see what happens ..."

ABOUT THE STORIES

Jack and the Beanstalk is a popular English fairy tale that was made into many film and TV adaptations. Similar tales about a boy who defeats a giant and acquires his wealth can be found in other parts of the world.

The Bean Tree contains elements from *Jack and the Bean Trees*, a tale from Appalachia in the eastern United States. I have combined these elements with the storyline from the earliest recorded version of *Jack and the Beanstalk*, published in 1807 by Benjamin Tabart as *History of Jack and the Bean-Stalk*. Here, Jack recovers what rightly belongs to him, rather than being a clever thief.

Olaf and the Troll is a based on a fairy tale called *Boots and the Troll* from Norway.

Molly and the Giant is a story that comes from Scotland, where it is known as *Molly Whuppie*. In contrast to the other stories, the main character is a girl.